KT-160-193

I'm just about to read my new book when . . .

"Albie!"

It's Mum.
"Time to go swimming,"
she says.

Swimming?
GREAT!

Outside, it's **pouring**.
Uh-oh!

Mum and I pull on our
boots and trudge through
the rain.

At the pool I leap into the water.
SPLOSH!

Down,
down,
down
I dive.

The pool gets darker, and colder and scarier.
Seaweed licks at my face in the murky gloom.

OOOOOOOH!
And what's THAT coming towards me?

It's a shark!
YIKES!

I swim for my life, but the shark opens its terrible jaws and swallows me whole.

WOOOAAAHHH!

I slither down the shark's throat . . .

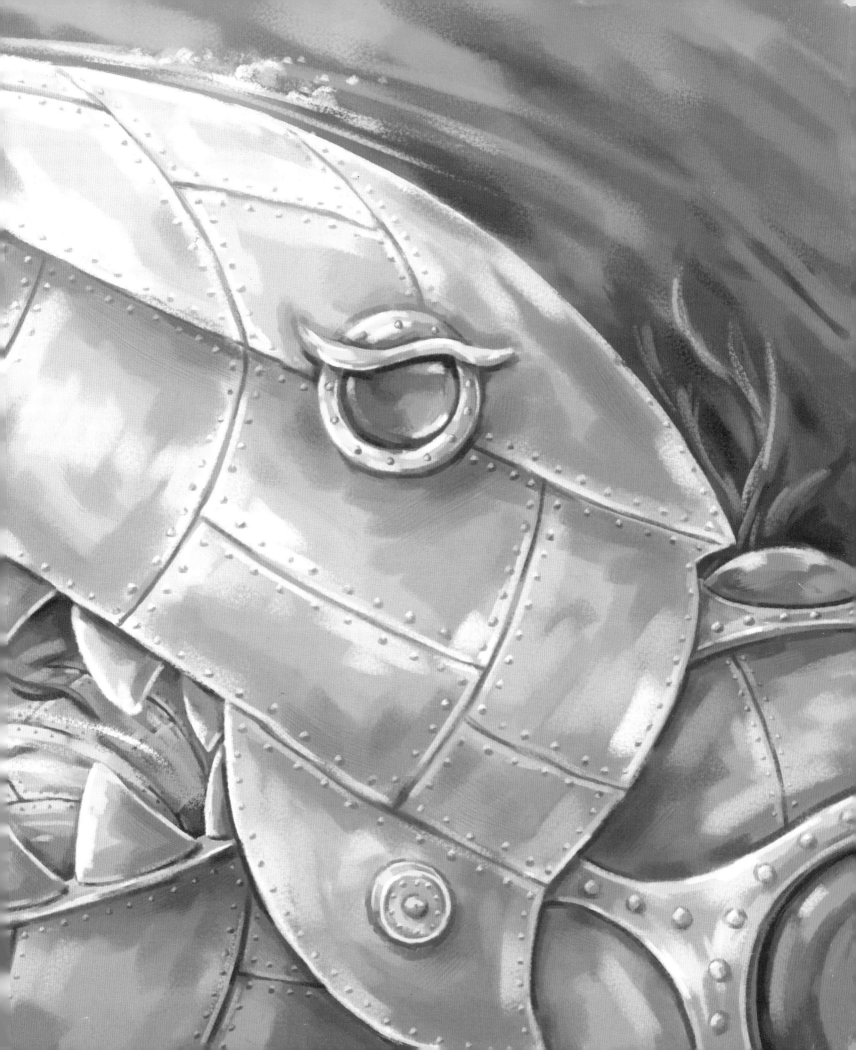

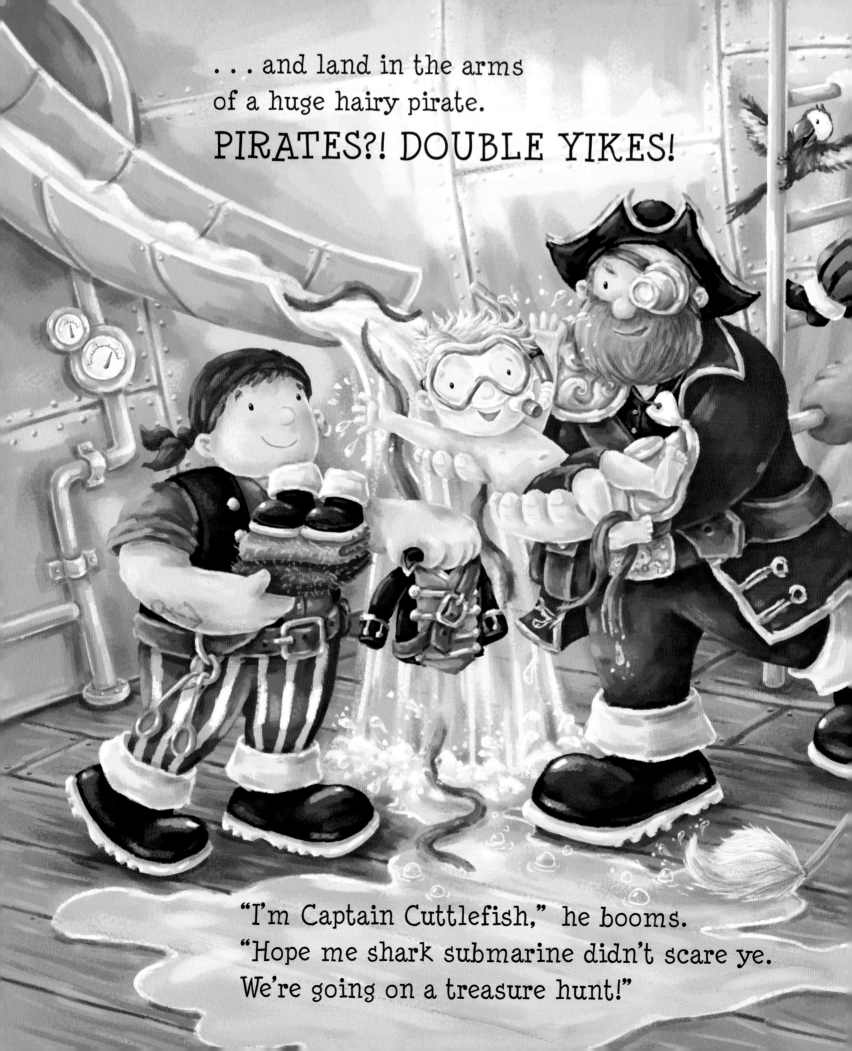

. . . and land in the arms
of a huge hairy pirate.
PIRATES?! DOUBLE YIKES!

"I'm Captain Cuttlefish," he booms.
"Hope me shark submarine didn't scare ye.
We're going on a treasure hunt!"

A treasure hunt? AWESOME.
He hands me the map and
WHOOSH!

We plunge straight into a
forest of seaweed. Uh-oh!
Suddenly...

AARRRGGGHH!

A hideous monster appears at the window!
It has enormous teeth, huge, googly eyes
and a glowing light dangling from its head.
"W-what's THAT?" I stammer.

"It's only Mabel," laughs the Captain.
"She's come to show us the way."

With Mabel's help, we weave our way
through the seaweed and out into a
maze of enormous boulders.
It's SO beautiful.
Then, one of the boulders **sneezes** . . .

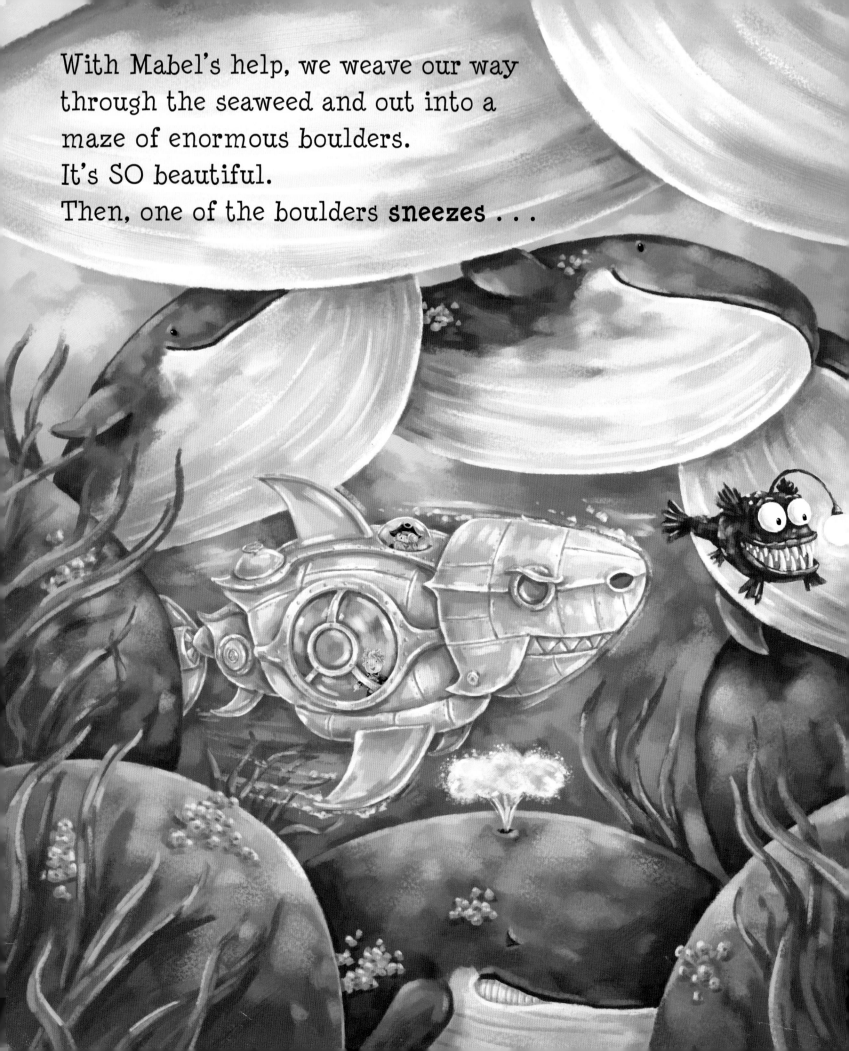

and we are carried up into the air
on a gigantic plume of water!

"There she blows!" laughs the Captain.

The whale lets us gently back down, next to the
wreck of a colossal ship.
"AHA!" chuckles the Captain. "That was lucky!"
We set off on our sea-scramblers to look for treasure.

Inside, it's dark and spooky. I have the strangest feeling we're being watched. Soon we find what we're looking for.

Unfortunately, something we are NOT
looking for finds US!
Uh-oh!

I zoom off on my sea-scrambler, but some seaweed gets caught in the engine, and I spin out of control! Round and round and round I whizz, stirring the water into a cloud of bubbles.

WOOOAAAHHH!

But I'm not the only one getting dizzy. When I finally come to a stop, the giant octopus is a mass of tangled tentacles.

HOORAY!
Now we can get the treasure!

Inside the treasure chest are piles and piles of glittering gold coins. But what's this? Nestled among the coins is something even more precious.

Six tiny octopus babies!
So that's what the giant
octopus was guarding!

Carefully, we scoop up the
babies and place them in
the Captain's hat.

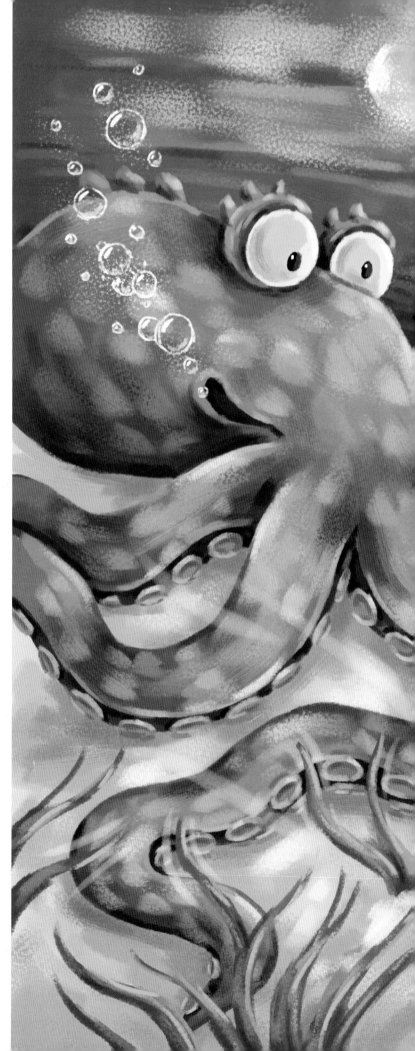

We swim to the octopus mother, untangle
her tentacles, and give her the babies.

Then we hurry back to the
submarine and head for home.

"Well done, young Albie-me-lad,"
beams Captain Cuttlefish.
"We couldn't 'ave done it without ye!"
"Thanks!" I grin. "I had a great time!"

The Captain winks, then hands me
a bag brimming with chocolate coins.
"Don't eat 'em all at once!" he laughs.

Back at the poolside, Mum is waiting. She hands me a towel.

"Come on, Albie," she says. "Let's go home and read your new book."